Aa

A is for Alfie and his little sister, Annie Rose.

B is for bedtime and blanket.

C is for Chessie, Alfie's black-and-white cat.

Dd

D is for drawing. Alfie is drawing a picture of Annie Rose.

D is also for door. (Be careful not to slam it!)

E E is for elephant. Alfie's
e elephant is nearly as old as Alfie.
He sleeps in Alfie's bed every night.

F is for friends. Alfie's best friend is Bernard.

Ff

Gg

G is for Grandma. She can dance and sing and tell stories.

H is for hat. This one's a bit too large for Alfie.

Hh

Ii

I is for the insects Alfie loves to find under rocks.

Jj

J is for jacket. In winter, Alfie stays warm in his red jacket.

Kk

K is for kitten.

This one is called Boots.

L is for lamb, Annie Rose's favourite toy.

M is for moon. A silver light, always changing shape. Magic moon.

Mm

N n

N is for neighbours. The MacNally family, who live across the street from Alfie, are very good neighbours indeed.

Oo

O is for "Open the door, Alfie."

P p

P is for park and puddles.

Qq

Q is for questions. Alfie is very good at
asking them. Luckily his friend Maureen
is good at answers.

R r

R is for reading. Maureen always reads Alfie
a story when she comes to baby-sit.

Ss

S is for seaside, swimming, and sand castles.

Tt

T is for tent, teatime, and teddies.

Uu

U is for umbrella, which makes a good tent too, even when it's not raining.

V v

V is for visit, like when Grandma
arrives in her little red car.

W is for water
(better outdoors than in!).

Ww

Xx

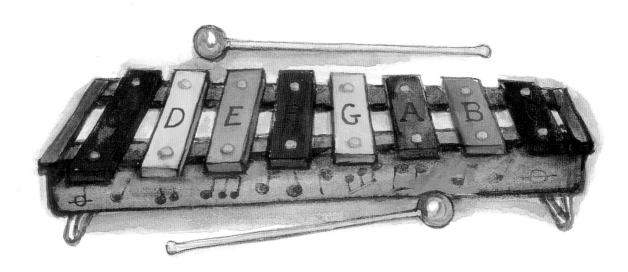

X is for Alfie's xylophone. Each bar has its own letter and makes a different sound when Alfie hits it.

Y is for yellow. Alfie is very pleased
with his new yellow boots.

Zz

Z is for zip . . .

and this is the end of Alfie's ABC.